THIRTEEN NIGHTS:
VIENNESE VARIATIONS

THIRTEEN NIGHTS:

VIENNESE VARIATIONS

EVA BIANCA

ANDALUS PUBLISHING

LOS ANGELES

Thirteen Nights: Viennese Variations
© 2015 Eva Bianca
Andalus Publishing
ISBN-13 978-0-9910476-8-0

Publisher's Cataloging-In-Publication Data:

Names: Bianca, Eva.

Title Thirteen nights : Viennese variations / Eva Bianca

Description: Los Angeles : Andalus Publishing, [2015]

Identifiers: ISBN: 978-0-9910476-8-0

Subjects: LCSH: Man-woman relationships--Fiction. | Married men-
            -Fiction. | Scientists--Fiction. | Redemption--Fiction. |
            Self-realization--Fiction. | Vienna (Austria)--Fiction. |
            Paris (France)--Fiction. | LCGFT: Romance fiction.

Classification: LCC: PS3602.I158 T55 2015 | DDC: 813/.6--dc23

You let me violate you, you let me desecrate you
You let me penetrate you, you let me complicate you
You can have my isolation, You can have my absence
of faith
Help me tear down my reason, help me become some-
body else
Help me I broke apart my insides, Help me the only
thing that works for me,

You get me closer to god
You get me closer to god

Trent Reznor,
Nine Inch Nails
Closer

Fall

I left for Cape Town, prepared for anything. Facing death down will do that for you. Not a month before leaving, my world had forever shifted on its axis. I had just moved back to the States. What began as a night of reunion with old friends ended with utter loss of control of every vestige of communication and mobility I had always taken as my birthright. I was diagnosed with a brain tumor. And while this is not a story about that evening or that diagnosis, it is only in that context that the events to come will achieve their true significance.

At first I was in such denial about the night I almost died, I didn't even remember it. I woke up in my bed, sore and confused. Lisa and Michelle were in my reading nook, sitting vigil. They eased me into reclamation of the prior night's horrific events. I sent them packing and crawled around my house, coming to grips with the facts of what had happened, grappling with the holes in my memory. I lay down on the floor, on the driveway, in the various places advertised by my bloodshed as places I had been during that dark night, reenacting and waiting for the experience to fill in. Gradually, it did.

Over the next few weeks, I resisted the suck of the medical machine. It pulled me to it, with complete disregard for my routines. The workers scheduling appointments expressed their unconscious bias that I was now a sick person, a person with nothing to do so important as to sit in a waiting room with countless other frightened people, held hostage by disjointed and unexplained symptoms. My mother had worked within that establishment during her long life and she had voiced nothing but disdain. My father, on the other hand, had teased his cancer into submission for years within that system, holding to the maxim that knowledge was power. Somewhere in between them would lay my truth. Linda, my childhood friend and chosen sister, was with me when the first neurosurgeon pronounced his sentence. "Possibly, six months without surgery; six–eight and paralysis to some degree, with." Wow. Life was no longer as we had known it.

I had planned to go to a conference in Cape Town for quite some time. The paper I was to present became my salvation. I poured myself into its writing and I decided to go on the trip anyway, come what may. It's funny how life works. One part of your existence can be completely unraveling while another is going gangbusters. I had test after test. I kept expecting to be told that everything was fine; it was all a big mistake. Instead, the most obscure anomalies were revealed. There were nodes here and masses there. Concurrently, I found myself presented with new unexpected opportunities from contacts that I was working with on projects. One of these was to attend some expert group meetings associated with a United Nations Working Group while at the Cape

Town conference. I accepted.

By that time I had settled on a neurosurgeon who was cautious and rational. He burned me a complete set of the scans of my beautiful brain and I left. And because I had a second conference in France three weeks later, I booked a ticket to Cape Town with a return to the States from Paris. The time in the middle was open to the wind.

I cannot tell you what it felt like those weeks prior to my trip. I can tell you what I was able to do and not do. I can tell you what I hung on to. I could not sleep. I was afraid to be in my house alone. I wrote and wrote and wrote in my journal. I ran. I ran whenever I could not sleep. I ran in the dark. I ran in the light. My life began to assume some new contours. I woke pre-dawn. I wrote in my journal. I ran. These were old friends, writing and running. I found a completely raw core person who had been dormant inside of me for years. This was the eight year-old girl who ran in the rain while her parents fought like the dickens. This was the twisted teen who penned her angst. Any tatters to my integrity I had suffered in the interim years quickly healed. By the time I left for South Africa I felt ready for whatever the universe would put before me.

Cape Town feels like it's at the bottom of the world. Maybe it's the position of the stars, so completely different from my usual perspective. When I arrived I was immediately caught up in my network, feeling more love than I thought possible from people I barely knew, and then only in a professional setting. I was completely forthcoming about my situation.

After several days of presentations and runs through idyllic parks with a colonial flair, I attended one of the meetings I had agreed to observe. By now I was feeling wonderful, grounded, plugged in, aware of happy possibilities. I sat in my seat, took stock of the room, saw many familiar faces. The meeting began.

And the door opened. A tall man stood there, phone at his ear. His eyes met mine with a smile. And he turned and walked out. My heart did that thing again. It woke back up.

The door opened again. This time, the man

gestured that he was going to come to sit in what appeared to be an empty seat next to me. I returned with a hand movement directing him to a different seat, across the table. There was a computer in the chair next to me. Better. I could look at him this way.

And he could look at me. He did. I knew he felt it too. I could see it and I could feel it at the same time that it was happening. The voices in the room were turning into so much droning background noise, like the sound of the grownups in Charlie Brown television specials. There, but completely incomprehensible. I had eyes, senses, for nothing but him.

I tried to take notes. Unintelligible. He was in the same condition. I was still feeling him. I knew what he was feeling because I was feeling it too. I could not take my eyes off of his hands.

I have no idea how long the meeting wore on. It could have been two hours, it could have been ten minutes. Time had no relevance. I was somewhere else. I knew when everyone left he would stay and talk to me. I was right.

I was chatting with a colleague and he came up

with a completely pre-textual excuse to get my card. So what. I gave it to him. And then he invited himself along to my dinner. I was going to the top of the adjacent hotel, to appreciate the view and grab a bite. We chatted happily.

When we sat down in the lounge to wait for a table, I just jumped in feet first. I had come to the decision, prior to my trip, that I should just tough out the next phase of my life by myself. It seemed best, brain tumor and all. Factor in a recent breakup and I felt like so much baggage. So, I told him precisely that. He was not shaken in the least. Instead, he said that he was almost divorced and wanted to be in my life in whatever capacity I would permit. A fireworks display shot off in the harbor. We sat to dinner. I couldn't eat.

When I got back to my hotel room, a lovely email awaited me. A dream evening. We made plans to see each other the next day.

I saw him a few more times before he left Cape Town to go home to Paris. Yes, Paris, where I was to end up on this walkabout. Our first physical contact came when we hugged one another and said so long as we made plans to see each other again there.

I had a lot of time to think after we parted company. My days were filled. I played tourist. I concocted a ritual and dropped my tumor in effigy to the bottom of the sea. After several glorious days, I hit the road, first visiting a good friend in Rome.

I had not been in Rome since the days immediately preceding the illness that ultimately felled my mother. I was still coming to terms with the realities of my divorce at the time, although it had been final for several years. Rome was at the end of a cruise through the Mediterranean and Adriatic Seas. I ended up going on it solo; according to the ship's bursar I was the only person on the ship with no association to anyone. Watching everyone from the outside, seeing the coupled-up nature of the herd, forced me to look at relationship from a different perspective than I had prior. By the time I got to Rome that year, I was full of questions and sorrow.

I would sit on the Spanish Steps and watch the lovers and the tourists and try to call my mother from pay phones while Hurricane Katrina headed for the South Florida coast. She never answered. Ultimately, days later, my youngest brother did. He had found my mother curled up in the fetal position in the center of her living room, on the top floor of her building, all the windows still ajar, completely unsecured against the storm. He was astonished that I was calling, as if that was my first call. I explained that I had been trying at near-hourly intervals for days. I changed my flight home. The next four months I took care of my mother, midwifing her for what was to come as she got ready to die.

And here I was, back on the Spanish Steps, now contemplating going home to deal with my own medical uncertainties. I thought about that time, and what I felt watching connected people while I was not. I realized that, all these years later, I finally felt connection. I thought about what could happen, if I was to have surgery and became paralyzed. I realized that I would not be able to live with myself if I didn't act upon my feelings, if I didn't allow myself to pursue whatever my heart felt to be right. I knew that

I would impose no restraints upon myself when I saw him next. I would allow my self beautiful connection and trust where it led.

Rome was madcap. Daniel, my expat friend, ran me ragged, literally and figuratively. We ran through ruins, we found and downed the most exotic shots imaginable. After a few days, I moved on to Brussels and a far more sedate visit with a dear girlfriend of mine. But by this time I had a firm date with him.

Maria and I decided on a fun shopping weekend Paris. She and I would arrive on Saturday and I would move on to Versailles, home to my conference, on Sunday. He would meet me at my hotel in Versailles. We would take it from there. I ran through the Luxembourg Gardens, shopped with Maria in Paris, and counted the hours till our meeting.

Until — the time was at hand. I walked into the lobby and there he was. How can I explain the next few days? Hours together? All told, they were few. But I had this feeling that I was living my destiny, that I could tell him anything, I could feel what he was going to say almost before he would say it.

He first kissed me on our walk back from a bistro that Sunday night, in the shadow of Versailles, full moon above. I will not go into the details of our passion, they remain ours and this is not that sort of story. But the feeling of absolute rightness, that I must share, along with the sense of profound connection and my feeling that we were transcending time and dimension. Too soon, the week was up and I had to go home.

So, I did. I went for my MRIs and finally got some good news. No, we could not be completely sure about the cellular makeup of my tumor but we could be reasonably sure that it posed no immediate harm and very possibly no harm at all. I made an executive decision to forego further exploration of the various other irregularities the diagnostic fishing expedition had unearthed.

He started sending me energy when I was going for my MRIs. I could feel it, it washed over me. I started sending mine back. Who needs to text when you have white light to send? Our telepathic visitations commenced.

I started getting on with the business of my life, working on a large project, and blocking out the next parts of my thesis. We kept in touch. And gradually, day by day, I began to realize just how much he meant to me. My living room was full of the remnants of my life in Montreal, those parts that had made the cut and the move back to Florida. We planned for a visit. As I worked to integrate my households, I slowly began the process of adjusting my long-held, nearly calcified boundaries to allow for his proposed arrival. Small things but telling. I put a reading light on the other side of my bed. He could have whichever side he wanted. Now, I could read on either as could he. Subtle but conscious choices.

I learned early on that he was not given to idle communication. There was no needy groping for constant affirmation. But the quality of the interaction we did enjoy was exquisite. He spoke my language. He could be naughty, he could be poetic. He seldom failed to respond to a significant detail. I shared some writing of mine, some parts of my soul, and waited for his response.

I often found myself in the unfamiliar role of waiting—for promised calls, or simple responses. And there were times when the connection was so acute and then so simply not there, that I lacked the emotional repertoire to interpret. What was this thing I felt? This disconnect? That initial deep seated certainty that I could tell him anything compelled me to call him out on his tendency to advance and retreat. It was more something I could sense since our interactions mainly consisted of telephone conversations and email letters, than something with concrete definition. But sense it I did, and tell him I had to. His response met me with the same degree of honesty. He promised me fidelity and depth of communication.

It became easier for us to reveal ourselves to each other. I continued to work on my project for the agency that had originally sent me to the meeting where we met. When I ultimately presented my research and my findings to them, I asked if it would be possible for me to participate further as a part of their country's delegation. They were enthusiastic and receptive, agreeing that it was a good idea and giving me enough of a green light that I began to investigate travel options. He was ecstatic. We could be together in Vienna. We started making plans. First, time in Vienna, then in Paris.

By now, we had admitted the depth and breadth of our feelings to ourselves and to one another. And we shared some dreams. He told me about a dream he had of me on a cruise ship, serene as I waited for him to return with a drink,both of us certain of the rightness of our union. I, too, had dreamed about him that week. But did I want to share my dream? It came with a heck of a backstory. He urged me to tell him and I did.

During the months after I returned from Rome years before, while I cared for my declining mother and dragged myself to work at the court 75 miles from her house every day,I felt like the joys my life would hold were all behind me. I had nothing extra, no joie de vivre, no lightness of being. It was all I could do to maintain my fearsome level of responsibility. My mother and I had never known an easy relationship. She resented me for a multitude of reasons about which I could do nothing — I was my father's daughter and his blood ran through my veins, I was an overachiever and therefore a disincentive for my brothers to strive for their dreams, I took care of myself hence I was vain. The service of caring for her on her terms in her home, despite the gross inconvenience, while she continued to snipe at me, was taking its toll.

My experiences on the cruise were still quite fresh — the feeling that I had let connection, my marriage, escape my clutches without enough of a fight. I wondered if I would go to my own grave never knowing intimacy again. One night, after a grueling week of drudgery, I had the most vivid dream. In it, I was at the court. There was a visiting judge, a man my age and like me in that he was vital and attractive and accomplished. We were friends, but no more. He was married. The dream was so vivid I woke up and wrote about it in my journal. I had known his name while I was asleep but as I regained full consciousness, it garbled. I wrote what I could remember—it was a Latin name but I knew that it was approximate.

I went back to sleep. I was back in that very vivid place, but now it was years later. I no longer worked at the court. I was somewhere academic, but it was not a law school or a university. Somehow, there was some affiliation with human rights. And my participation was informal, I was not lecturing or presenting, but I was there. I was talking to a man and we were discussing health issues. He invited me to dinner, we fell in love, and after some time, we were together. Forever.

When I woke up, I thought about it. I assumed it was the same man, the judge, and I assumed it was his wife's illness we had discussed since we then went to dinner and continued with our lives together. I felt edified by this dream at a hopeless time. I knew that there was someone out there like myself, someone who would get me on those deeper levels, and I could hunker down and be patient. I no longer worried about my fate. It would take care of itself. I told my daughter and all of my friends about the dream. It was a sign, a portent.

And three weeks later, I met the judge I had dreamed about. He looked exactly the same, as I had imagined. True, I had the syllables of his name transposed, but I had a sense of that as I wrote them. There he was, in the flesh, physical affirmation that my dream had somehow tapped into some underlying metaphysical vein of possibility. I asked the judge for whom I worked to inquire as to his marital status. When it turned out that he was married, I was a bit astonished and almost ecstatic. Over the years, we ran into one another several times. He was always a perfect gentleman. I was always a perfect lady. I doubt he had the slightest inkling that I had ever had a dream about him prior to our meeting. Nothing ever happened between us.

But back to the dream about my man...Over the years, I wondered what that dream meant. Did it mean that someday the judge and I would find our way to each other? Or did it just mean that I should not give up and never settle? I went on with my life.

Now, in the present, I had a dream about my new friend and the judge. We were in a house by the sea, the three of us splayed on a daybed, in a half-dressed menage à trois. As the judge made overtures toward me, I turned to my man, nestled in his arms feeling absolute safety. I looked at the judge and told him that I was following my heart. The sun came out in my man's smile.

As I ran that morning, after waking, the import of the dream hit me full on. I realized that my old dream was allowing space for my new reality. I realized that the first dream from so long ago had actually been two dreams - the one about the judge and then the one about the man with whom I went to dinner. And, I realized that the academic situation with connections to human rights could very well be the UN meeting where I met my friend. With whom I discussed a health situation—mine—at dinner.

I shared all of this with him, not quite sure of an expected reaction. But, as always, I showed up all the way—I just spoke my truth. And he quietly told me that he believed in dreams and that he was falling in love with me.

From that moment on, I thought of him as

the man of my dream, my soul mate, the person for whom I had been waiting season after season. *Besherte.* Meant to be. I told him that I believed that we would someday be together, all the way.

Holidays

Christmas was upon us. We were far from each other with my eyes open, but always together when I closed them. Then, he was in the next room. We took each other on a photojournalistic tour of our holiday preparations. He sent me pictures of scenes from Parisienne streets, with his essays attached explaining his reflections. Our Viennese reunion was getting closer. What was a little more time in the big picture?

He was going to spend Christmas with his mother. His two daughters would join them for a visit immediately after the big day and then the three of them would head back to Paris. During his week in the country at his mother's, we were not able to stay in the close touch we had come to enjoy and I felt it again, that strange disconnect. What was that? I realized that this was what truly missing someone felt like. Not mental missing, but an actual disconnect of the heart.

I turned to music. I pored through my library, looking for songs and pieces that expressed my feelings for him. As the days wore on, the compilation changed in nature. I expanded it to include old favorites and songs that had shaped my human experience. From there, I moved into songs about endurance and longing and missing. Some things made it in on pure intuition. I played the ever-growing amalgam constantly—while decorating, then entertaining, while preparing for my annual pig roast. I played it in the house, in my yard, in my car, I played it on my iPod. My friends had different reactions to the whole musical gift extravaganza. Some asked for copies. Others, aware of the implications of some offerings, were concerned that I was laying myself bare, vulnerable for great hurt.

And with the music I wrote out a key, explaining some of my choices. I felt that if he loved me as he did so far, this could only open the door for him to love and appreciate me even more. I was giving him a large chunk of my musical experience beginning with my early Beatles infatuation. My life in music.

I never told him what his Christmas gift was, preferring the element of surprise. Instead, I alluded to the fact that it was controversial and very custom made. I couldn't wait to give it to him, hopefully in person. I wanted to listen to it with him. I continued to listen to it myself, always ending up in tears. It made me feel connected to him while he was off the grid.

And then he was back in Paris and back in touch. Glorious connection. We made our hopeful promises to each other about the coming year and sent New Years pictures.

Winter

He had played with the idea that he could take a few days and come to see me prior to Vienna. I didn't really mind waiting the extra time. We had waited that long and I thoroughly appreciated the demands upon his time. However, I very much wanted some quiet time, in personal surroundings, where we could just be together. I wanted to share with him the unique serenity of my property, the chimes on my lanai, the night-blooming jasmine, the beauty of a well-built fire. The idea of kitchen collaboration was seductive in its domestic simplicity. I hoped that he could put it together.

The day his older daughter went back to university, we spoke for a long time, about love and fidelity and each other. He sent me a beautiful drawing by Hiroshige, with his letter attached describing it and his feelings for me, for us. The next day he would attend an important meeting and find out whether his schedule would permit a visit pre-Vienna. More waiting, the only offset to a nearly feline sense of complacency.

I woke that Monday with a sense of foreboding. I couldn't shake it. Something felt off. My familiar ministrations could not pull me into my day's activities. I worked on my breathing, thrown by the nearly physical sense of a shift beneath the surface. I checked my emails and my travel arrangements for the upcoming trip to Vienna, now only 3 1/2 weeks away, and learned that my plans were awry. Red lights. I felt a chill. My flight wasn't booked. My hotel reservation in Paris was, for some unknown reason, canceled. I continued to wait.

Mid-day, he sent an email, curt, to the point. His work responsibilities would preclude a visit. There.

That was done. I had never really expected him to come. But, still, the ominous undercurrent pervaded. Why did he not call to tell me? I sent a lengthy email, expressing my disappointment and resignation and continued with my day. Living with a brain tumor was teaching me acceptance of circumstances outside of my control, my responsibility for positive engagement with my present, regardless of outcomes.

Tuesday, I woke to a lovely message of support. Things would not always be thus. The passage of time would help ease the constraints that kept us apart. My senses remained alert. Something still was not right. I called him.

For the first time, communication was uneasy. I had the distinct impression that he didn't understand anything I was trying to say. I wanted to talk about Vienna, and his expectations and mine. I wanted to make sure that we were on the same page. This was a professional milieu that, for the first time, I would be integrating with a very personal relationship. I did not want to commit career suicide. But he did not really hear me, or my concerns. I felt the bottom start to fall out.

And then I opened my email. I had one from the agency that had so rallied at the idea of my inclusion as a part of the delegation to the UN meetings in Vienna in February. My participation at this time was now thought to be premature. Red light.

I forwarded the email to him, hoping that he would be able to help me understand the subtle diplomatic implications of my situation because of his advanced experience in these matters. No response.

Wednesday, I woke to a brief one line email. He understood my situation. Could he call me that afternoon? So formal. I could not relax. I forced myself to work. I made a list of talking points for our conversation, the issues that I had most felt he misunderstood the day before. I waited.

The minute I heard his voice, I knew. I heard the "but" before he said it. He loves me. He never meant to be a destructive influence in my life. If stress he brought into my life caused me trouble with my tumor, he could not live with himself. His life was unbalanced. His younger daughter was going through an extremely rough time. She lives with him, counted on him completely, and things were out of whack with her. He could not bring me into this mess. It would not be fair to me. He would always be with me, we would see each other again, but we could not be together now. Do not come to Vienna. Do not come to Paris. All I could hear was his cop out. And yet, in my heart of hearts, I did not believe we were truly over.

I told him what a mistake I thought he was making, that together we could face anything. I had been a troubled teen. I had insight. I could help. He sounded awful, depleted of the joy I had come to associate with him, his voice, his spirit. He promised to call me the next day to continue our conversation.

But he didn't. Thursday came and went. No call. I sent him emails of support. I wrote him a poem and sent that too. I waited. I was devastated. Instead, late Thursday I received a beautiful email, outlining his feelings for me, their depth, his sadness, that his life was complex and difficult. His was a completely unilateral decision. My feelings, my opinion, my position, mattered not at all. The email ended by saying that he would call the following day—Friday.

And Friday came and went. No call. I sent him the flash drive containing his music compilation, his Christmas present. Who knew if and when I would see him again? By now I had reached out to my friends. To my surprise, save for Lisa, Ben and my brother David, they all threw him, me, us, under the bus. "What did you expect? You hardly knew each other since he lives so far away. You loved each other after knowing one another only a few months." I had a brain tumor. They asked me what kind of judgment I could possibly have, given my brain tumor?

I got hammered Friday night and succumbed to doubt. Why hadn't the bastard called? Then, a full-body massage Saturday afternoon, and by Sunday I had worked myself back to a zen place of acceptance. Radio silence. I gave him a heads up about the imminent arrival of his gift and its personal nature. He doesn't open his own mail. Do unto others...and I asked about his failure to respond to my emails.

And just when I least expected it, there was an

email from him, telling me that I was beautiful in every way, that he knew I came from a pure, loving place, and that he would answer my emails always. His mother had unexpectedly taken ill. That is why he did not call on Friday. I sent him a message of support.

His mother's situation worsened. His work commitments pressed on. His daughter needed his constant help. Providing him encouragement became my mission for the next three weeks. I never broached the subject of Vienna. I had made other arrangements. I would go as the representative of an NGO with permanent observer status. Although I would be limited in the ways I could participate, my thesis would still benefit from the observation of public international rule-making at this level. I put the idea of seeing him in the hands of the Great Other. I lit a candle with two wicks for us.

Every day I sent him some light, some support, my love, but I refrained from using the L word. He was warm and appreciative and receptive. My hope stirred. We continued to write, but he never called. Not once. I visited New Orleans with Lisa and included him in the trip with pictures and videos and our electronic banter nearly assumed the ease of days yore. He commented that I looked stunning in a picture that I shared. He was not immune to my charms. Hope.

He continued to write me from different locations on his work trips, most often from trains to and from Paris, always expressing his gratitude for my love and support. Thank you thank you thank you. And suddenly, I sensed a shift in tone in his correspondence. Where once he had been open, accessible, revealing, now he was merely informative and closed. We had achieved the tedium of small talk. I stopped my daily affirmation campaign. I felt myself approaching some modern day fine line between eternal support and stalking. But, when true inspiration moved me, I would hit send. And he continued to reply, although the subtle distance was becoming more apparent to me.

Vienna

Day One

I got to Vienna. I had been to the city before, but never in winter. He sent me an e-mail in response to a picture I had sent from NYC the day prior. I lay in the snow and took a picture of Stephansdom, lit by another full moon, to let him know I had arrived in Austria.

When he and I had planned the trip together, I had booked myself into a hostel as backup. I was not comfortable with the idea of staying in his room as my primary place of residence during the meetings. I had never stayed in a hostel before but I had a colleague and dear friend who had often done so and he spoke so glowingly of his experiences and had helped me pick out a suitable place. I was so grateful that I had made these standby arrangements. My hostel was warm and welcoming, particularly in the bitter February chill.

My room was small, scrupulously clean, and spartan. It reminded me of a time long before when I had lived on a yacht. There was just enough space to put my things. I had only what I needed, no more. Tomorrow was the first day of the UN meetings. This was the culmination of so much that I had strived toward for so long. In addition to the reality that he could, very possibly would, show up, I was living the actualization of this long-cherished professional dream. Would I be able to sleep?

I snuggled in my cozy little bed, glad for the heat, and started to drift. And felt myself falling through space, my limbs completely paralyzed, unable to even turn my head. I kept falling. A massive weight pinned me to the mattress.

Night One

She got up and looked at her clothes, hanging in the small closet. So many choices, so little time. Today was the day! Anything was possible, anything could happen. First day of plenary. And Philippe might come!!! True, they hadn't spoken of it, but that just made it all the better. She picked her clothes with care. Something that showed her curves without being too obvious. Subtle but edgy. And, of course, her fur. Surely, when he saw her he would remember her comments about making love on top of it!

She trudged to the U-Bahn in the snow after a cheery farewell to the staff at the front desk. They all knew of her excitement. Everyone who knew her knew how much she loved Philippe, how excited she was at the prospect of seeing him again. Eva knew, in her heart of hearts, that this was the right way to handle it. No pressure. It had been best not to speak to him of her trip. He had so much on his plate, so much to deal with. It would be so much better to be a happy surprise for him.

She got to the UN and the pass office. The picture on her credentials came out a bit funny - the photographer caught her in mid-flirtation. She found her way to the meeting room and her seat at the table as representative of the NGO. Looking around, she scoped out Philippe's place in the room. It was just down the row from hers. He would be so close!

"Eva, you're here!" "Hello, are you here from Montreal or Florida?" "Are you done with your PhD yet?" "You look wonderful!" She was feeling the love.

And then she felt the air in the room change. He was here. She knew it without turning around. He walked in back of her, over to his place further down the table, phone at his ear, still unaware of her presence. Eva sat very still. She was getting good at waiting. And then he looked over. The sun came out. His face lit up. he gestured madly. Meet him by the coffee machine. She did.

They were transfixed with one another, laughing and happy. They stole kisses in a stairwell, glad to be reunited and all was right with the world.

∽∽∽

Day Two

First day of the meetings and I was working on getting my bearings. I couldn't run because of the ice and snow in the streets. This was not good. I got myself to the UN, got my credentials, and found my place. It was a long day, full of procedural formality. Every time the door opened, my heart lifted. Every time I saw who it was not, it fell.

There was a reception that evening and I made dinner plans with a colleague. While dining, I received an email from him. I was ecstatic. He wasn't in Vienna, but I had let him know I was and, although he did not directly respond to that information, he was responding to me. I wrote back.

Night Two

Head on pillow, calming my thoughts, and again, falling, falling, falling, until I am stuck and cannot move.

Philippe is on the phone. Again. Always. It doesn't

stop ringing. She can hear it. She can see it. The hospital. Work. His daughter. Please. He is rushing home now, trying to figure out how to delegate, how to calm, how to manage. Enough already.

∽∽∽

Day Three

The plenary droned on. I took notes and watched and listened. A fly on the wall. His alternate showed up, not him. What could that mean? After a party at the German ambassador's residence that evening, I found my way home to the hostel in the snow. My spirits were flagging.

Night Three

I tried to go to sleep but the situation was starting to wear on me. I had this nagging sensation that something was not right. He had not responded to me. I sent an old picture, of a double rainbow, that had, once upon a time, evoked a happy response from him. Nothing. I could not stop my rumination. My mind continually went over every interaction from January forward, in scrupulous detail. Was he okay? Was his mother okay? Was his daughter okay? Had I done something? Had my decision to come to Vienna, after he had told me not to, somehow turned him against me?

By now I had ascertained that his presence at this particular meeting was of no great import. He did not need to be in Vienna. Perhaps he had delegated the task because he wanted to avoid me? Or was it something worse? No matter what, I knew he was not coming. I just knew.

I tossed and I turned. I never slept. But, thankfully, that night I was spared an alternate reality where I was forced to endure an unverifiable version of events.

~~~

Day Four

Again, I fixed myself up and put on my game face, ready for another day at the races. What had loomed before me as a wonderful opportunity to learn, to network, was proving to be a test of endurance. I had gone several days without sleep and without running. I was dealing with snow and ice, my least favorite elements, coupled with public transportation. I had the wrong footwear. I lived in fear of a slip on the ice. I never said his name. I never let slip my personal hell, but anyone who knew me, who had ever experienced my effervescent charm, knew that something was drastically wrong. I went to work anyway.

I stood in the hallway and called him, leaving a long message telling him that I was wrapping my head around the reality that he was not going to be in Vienna for this round of meetings. My voice broke as I left the message, as I told him that time had done nothing to assuage my feelings. I expressed my deep desire to speak to him. I rambled. It was the first time I had spoke of anything other than my support since the day, a month before, when he told me we could not be together at this juncture.

Night Four

Meanwhile, I was developing a love/hate relationship with Room 7 in my hostel. The hostel itself was wonderful — collegial, full of life and music and warm staff who listened to my sad tale with unfathomable patience. Room 7, on the other hand, was both my refuge from the storm and my prison. I could not wait to get back to my solitude, where I could let myself cry, wail, but the loathsome reality of the hours that I would have there alone, unable to sleep? That was becoming torture. However, try to sleep I did.

Again, I put my head down. I worked on my breathing, I meditated. I fell asleep. Sort of...

Philippe sat at his desk, looking at his email inbox, frowning. Would this bitch ever stop? What the hell had he been thinking? I mean, she seemed like a nice enough girl but this was out of control. All of those emails. He had thrown her a bone, told her about his ailing mother just to ease the let down of the break up.

Then, he got the call from the mail room. That's right, she said she sent him something. Well, she appeared to have good taste. Maybe it was something decent. No harm in checking it out. After the massive inconvenience of going to the mail facility, housed in a separate structure from headquarters, this was what she had sent him? A flash drive? With this bizarre assortment of music? How many renditions of "Summertime" and "Somewhere Over the Rainbow" did one person need? As if anyone needed any of that sappy nonsense. Dear God, and what was with the flipping love songs? One after the other, Cole Porter, Gershwin, jeez. Nine Inch Nails "Closer"? This chick had it bad.

What was he going to do? Clearly, he could not get rid of her if he was civil. She was like a sweet little puppy dog — if you were nice it would never go away.

Kick it and it would just think you slipped. No, the only thing to do was cut her off cold. Like it had never happened. She would get it. Eventually. They always did. And he wouldn't have to know about it. He would just route her emails to spam and block her number on his phone. Like it had never happened.

Day Five

By now, the expert groups were in full swing. I was doing my best to stay engaged in discussion, to follow the activity, but it was a struggle. My mind was jumping around. I was having trouble eating. And sleep was a memory. Still, I went out with colleagues, attempting to be social, to keep up some vestiges of normalcy. I was a flop. I knew better than to drink. I left early, by myself, took a tram the wrong direction, and got lost in an industrial part of town, long after midnight. I had visions of myself just dropping in the snow, out of sheer and utter exhaustion, to be found at some point in the future, frozen dead, swathed in my beautiful mink coat.

Night Five

Room 7. Home. I found it. After the perils of getting there, I did not know what else the night could bring...

Philippe was back in the same hotel in Warsaw. He had been spending too many nights there this winter, working on this project, not yet able to bring it to close. What a long tedious winter it was. His life had become a blur of airports and train stations, the hospital, his office, his apartment, the meeting rooms in this cold city, and this hotel. He signaled the bartender. She brought him another glass of wine. She was pleasant.

So much decay. The hospital was full of it. It smelled different. It started to cling to your skin. It was hard to see the changes in his mother. It hurt.

The girl smiled at him. She was young. No decay

there. He smiled back. They started talking.
And one thing led to another.

᠁᠁᠁

Day Six

By now the days were losing any distinction, one from another. I was the living dead. I had plans to explore some of Vienna's finest art collections with a friend and colleague. His company was a delightful distraction, but the pressure of avoiding personal discussion of my obvious personal distress from this person who also knew him, was almost too much. I decided to stay in the hostel that evening, to pick up rations and cook my dinner in the lovely communal kitchen. The fact that I could not feel him, that I could not sense him, was as, if not more, disturbing than his silence. We had gone this many days without communicating before. Just. But never had I felt such absence. He was not with me.

Night Six

Why did I even turn off the light at this point? I lay in my bed and cried, hoping that exhaustion would carry me away. Instead...

Philippe looked over at his wife. She was still beautiful, twenty years and two kids later. He knew he was a lucky guy. Sure, she could be impetuous and yes, his constant traveling created challenges. And they would just have to agree to disagree about their approaches to the girls. But, he knew what he had.

That was a pretty stupid move he made back in October. The girl was interesting and yes, there were sparks flying. But he never thought she would be so persistent. After October, it had simply been an electronic flirtation. That was all. He had never given her any personal information - only a work email, a work cell phone, no Skype, no home address. Texting was minimal. Less that could incriminate him. He thought her health stuff would preoccupy her once she went back to the States. He hoped she would not pose a threat to his solid home life. The only thing to do was to cut her off cold turkey.

༄༄༄

Day Seven

I could not shake the horrible thoughts I felt welling up inside me. Labeling time as day or night was arbitrary for me. There was no longer much difference. My consciousness was severely altered. He could not possibly have loved me if he could cut me off so abruptly. I went out with my friends, to see the *Spanische Hofreitschule*, the Spanish Court Riding-School, but I excused myself from the balance of the day's plan and slunk back to Room 7.

I watched a movie and tried to organize my thoughts to no avail. It had been over a week since I had slept and over a week since I had run. My routines were completely obliterated. I tried to conjure up his face, his being, but I could not. He was not reachable. Still, I found myself trying. I sent a banal email, half-heartedly hoping to send some good cheer, to somehow change the dynamic between us.

Night Seven

Lying pinned to my rack, staring up at the ceiling in the dark, unable to move, lost in some parallel universe where my mind compulsively churned out reasons, explanations for the incomprehensible. I was completely stuck.

When he saw the agency email denying her entree as a member of the delegation, his canny sense of survival told him to extricate himself. She was a student. She was probably looking to him to help her. No way.

Day Eight

Much of the plenary was aflutter about an accomplishment of his agency. Overhead screens were devoted to streams of live information. When it was clear that his mission was a complete success, I texted him my congratulations. I did not even know why. It just seemed like a gracious thing to do. I was going through the motions.

Night Eight

Philippe had not spent so much time in Bordeaux since university. This was tough. Thank God for his daughter. And thank God for Eva. She was so sweet, so positive. She kept sending him inspiration. His mother was still in cardiac intensive care, but she was showing improvement and she had immense spirit. The challenge lay in navigating the medical support system, from a distance, and this while handling his career and parenting his teen.

The hospital had a good network set up, though, and today he was meeting with the head of Social Services to find out what programs were available for at-home help, both medical and domestic, for the time, in future, when his mom could leave the hospital. Her life would never be as it had been.

And what a surprise! The woman running the show was Birgitte, his girlfriend from undergraduate days. Small world. She was a welcome ray of sunshine in the confusing morass of paperwork and diagnoses. They made dinner plans. Eva was sweet, but she was far. Birgitte was here.

∽∽∽

Day Nine

The problem with all of these scenarios was their plausibility. I had no way to find out if any of them were true, no way to disembowel their toxic power. It was Valentines Day and I dressed up, in yet another chic outfit, and put on a brave face. But seriously, I just wanted to kill someone.

I was disgusted with the whole idea of love, of trust. For years, I had compartmentalized my emotions and my passion, only giving full vent in completely random situations with no chance of intrusion into my head, my heart, my reality. Now, I was reminded why. Affirmation.

I went to the UN anyway and tried hurling cynical invective in my lame attempt to declaw the holiday. Eventually, my buddy Mike and I left, playing hooky, and went over to the Belvedere and Klimt. But *The Kiss* threw me down a tunnel of despair, crashed me against the rocks. Seeing the lovers, their hands enmeshed, locked in embrace, reminded me of the Hiroshige and I had to look out the window for almost ten minutes trying to compose myself.

The fact of our disconnect haunted me. I declined Mike's dinner invitation and crawled home to Room 7 in the snow.

Night Nine

So, that was it. At the end of the day, after all the chaos of the five weeks preceding, it came down to this. Her body just could not go on. It was such an anti-climax, after so much manic activity. Exhausting, but distracting and deceptive; planning for details gave one the sense that you had any say at all in the ultimate outcome. But, truly he didn't. She died anyway.

Philippe was exhausted. How was he going to get through all of this? There was really no one but him. So much for family solidarity. Sure, for pictures and dinners, but not for the tough stuff. All he wanted to do was sleep. He stopped looking at his emails. He stopped going to work. It was all he could do to make sure his daughter went to school. One day at a time.

ഗ്രഗ്രഗ

Day Ten

I don't know what time my day started because the day before never ended. I was paralyzed by my preceding night's vision. It chilled me to the bone. I could not separate my projections from my perceptions at this point. I was too far gone from lack of sleep and lack of endorphins. But I was beginning to intuit that his silence did not have to be an all or nothing proposition. The fact of his abandonment might not necessarily completely undo the fact of his love, or at least his prior love, for me. Sometimes doubt can be positive. Sometimes it leaves room for truths as yet not contemplated. For all that, I did not pick up the phone and call him. I don't know why. I didn't trust myself. I knew I was a wreck. I knew he was dealing with imbalance from other sectors. Surely, he did not need any from me. And clearly, he did not want anything from me at all. He knew how to find me. And he chose not to. I chose to respect that. Check.

I began to think about what to do with myself once the meetings came to an end, several days hence. I had originally left the weekend open to visit my friend Piotr in Slovakia, thinking my love and I could use some time apart after several weeks of prolonged togetherness in Vienna. I took the decision to proceed with that plan and contacted my friend. But, I decided to check myself into a hotel instead of taking Piotr up on his kind offer to stay with him. I needed some privacy, in case these sleepless nights continued, and a rockstar bathroom — it was time to get myself in hand, to get myself back to beautiful. I needed to luxuriate in a large tub and soak this pain away.

The expert group meetings had wrapped up and I used the balance of the day making my travel arrangements on the Internet. Trains, planes, and automobiles. I was hitting the road. At least this chapter was coming to a close. Nothing lasts forever. That can be a very good thing.

I went to a presentation and reception at a think tank associated with the UN meetings. They slogged on far longer than I had expected and my patience was non-existent. I excused myself and took the U-Bahn to Stephansplatz where I found myself a trattoria full of opera patrons coming from the big Opera Ball, dressed in their finery, relaxed and happy and glamorous. I looked anything but. However, my coat was currency the maitre d' understood and he quickly seated me with a conciliatory flourish. I postponed my trek home to Room 7 as long as I could.

I tried changing my position in the small bed. Perhaps if I put my head in a different place the *feng shui* would save me from myself. It made reading more difficult so I watched a movie instead. I started to drift and I thought about my breathing. Feel the breath come in, feel the breath go out. It calmed me, grounded me, helped me stay right here right now. Whether it would last beyond the next breath was immaterial. I had the calm of that breath and then the next breath. I relaxed for a brief time but it did not last. Instead, I succumbed to my churning thoughts. I let them carry me back to the split-second moments in time where the rift between us might have occurred. I thought about the various scenarios my overactive subconscious had unhappily provided to me over the week and a half I had lay in this bed.

Night Ten

Overhauling IT was a big job, requiring attention to detail. Agathe did not ordinarily concern herself with the people associated with the different POP accounts she was tasked with managing. However, she had taken it upon herself to find out about the tall man early in November, when she was first assigned to this job. There was something so lighthearted and friendly about the way he greeted everyone, despite his level of responsibility.

She did something verboten. She started peeking at his e-mail account. He had a lot of e-mails from the same address and it was clearly not a professional address at that. She couldn't resist. She took a look. Wow. These were hot. Sometimes they were over her head. They weren't in C-language, and her English wasn't that good. But, she got the gist. They were something she might never receive. And she saw the woman's pictures. She was older, probably almost twice her age, but thinner than she would ever be. Bitch. And her life looked like too much fun. Racing around on boats? Traveling? Drinking shots? Dinner parties? Life is unfair.

But there are little things a girl can do to even up the score. She could route emails from that address into the ether. Why not? If he figured it out, it was a glitch. If he didn't, oh well. She had noticed that he wasn't sending much back to the woman for a few weeks. Maybe Agathe would be doing him a favor.

Philippe could not figure out why he had stopped receiving any communication from Eva at all. No more phone calls, no messages, no emails. Nothing. It was so unlike her. She had always been so constant, so loyal, so there for him.

And now, when he really needed her the most, she was gone. He supposed he deserved it. He had broken things off with her. He really had nothing to offer her at this point in time. His life was a mess. He couldn't be much of a lover, much less life partner. She was vivacious, beautiful. Hadn't she said that she could be with someone new within 72 hours if she chose? He didn't doubt it. The noble thing to do was respect her wishes and go quietly into the night.

ᗧᗧᗧ

Day Eleven

I got up completely pissed off — at myself for ever giving him even the time of day, at him for being a total disappointment, at Vienna for being cold and snowy.

I decided to run in the snow anyway. What the hell. If I fell down, so what. Maybe if I could get one part of my routine back, running, the other part, sleeping, would follow. Desperate measures for desperate times. Against the advice of the front desk, I stepped out into the cruel 0600 cold, bitter and bone-chilling. The flakes were coming down. I felt defiant. Bring it on.

I did my stretches and stepped off the curb. I got about .25 km, breathing in the flakes, hoping that my inner body heat would notch up and work in my favor, and I started coughing. It felt like whooping cough. The snow flakes were freezing my lungs. I turned around, defeated, and went back to get ready for the day.

I could not shake my anger. What the hell was this? Cut and run? He was either a chicken-shit asshole or a heartless asshole, but either way he was an asshole. He could not just tell me to go away? I had to go through all of these machinations? What had I done, other than love him and give him some music? This was completely irresponsible. And terrible karma. He had daughters. Didn't he realize that if you did this to one of us, you did this to all of us?

He could so easily put me out of my misery. But he did not.

After dinner with colleagues, I returned to my room.

I closed my eyes. The familiar sensation of falling through space returned. I was back in that place where everything was so poignantly alive and real I could not discern fantasy from reality. I was back reliving everything that had occurred from that fateful January phone call, our last, forward in time.

I heard the subtle nuances of his voice. I heard his own torture. I heard his ambivalence. I heard his sincerity. I heard how very much he wanted to do the right thing, how completely in denial he was about his motivations to get away from me.

Night Eleven

He looked at the phone. He had just hung up with her. It was all too much. Yes, he loved her. She made him come alive, something he had once wondered if he would ever feel again. She made him laugh, she made him think. She was beautiful and real and true. He wanted her. But he just could not bring himself to see her. Seeing her, going forward with her, admitting to himself that he was really in something with her, would seal the deal on the fact and finality of the absolute end of his marriage. And, the bottom line was, he was sad, so sad, about that. Allowing in that joy and laughter felt almost disrespectful to the vows he had made to his soon-to-be ex-wife.

Besides, these were his problems, his responsibilities. He could not involve her in things to do with his kid. That really felt like a betrayal of his marriage. And his daughter, she clearly had mixed feelings about Eva, running more to negative. Did Eva deserve to deal with adolescent anger? She had her own challenges.

If he called her, if he had to hear her voice full of

*tears and pain, it would break his heart. He could not
do that. It had seemed so simple back in Cape Town
and Versailles. So simple and so easy. He saw her, knew
what she was made of, knew his marriage was ending,
and figured that was the long and short of it. Eva was
the one that said it was sometimes not that simple, that
it felt very different, for people who take commitment
seriously, when you get to the point of no turning back,
when you realize that you will not spend your life with
that dear person. Your history has expired.*

*Philippe continued to look at the phone. If he left
her alone, did not encourage her, maybe she would get
on with her life. She had called him on his tendency
to advance and retreat. He could not bring himself to
tell her good-bye. He hoped that someday they would
run into each other and then, insha'Allah, if no one
else had come along for either, they could see. But not
now. What could he possibly say to her now?*

∽∽∽

Day Twelve

I began getting ready for work with a completely different attitude than the day before. No, I had not slept. But somehow the night's parallel reality had resonated with more truth than those previous. Thinking about his voice, and going over his words in his letters, was empirical data. I had my perceptions. I had to start with them. I might not be able to fill in the blanks for him, but I could dig deeper and really lock onto what I had thought and felt at the time that things transpired and I could really look at his words and dispense with my wishful thinking. Just see his words for what they said, the plain meaning. It was a better place to begin. And, at least I knew I was not a source of stress in his life.

I didn't feel the complete disconnect of the pre- ceding week or so, but I felt a stirring of something. I asked the universe to give me a sign. I knew that I would surely lose my sanity if I stayed locked in with all of my mind's fantastic attempts to complete this puzzle. I had to look outside of myself. I could not be a closed loop. I had to open up. Surely, there would be lessons here. Clues were everywhere.

And I was not disappointed. As I passed through security at the UN, removing my belongings from the bin I saw a miniature figure of an angel. I picked it up. It looked like a Fiorucci angel I had on a tee shirt eons ago. I asked the guard if I could have it and she smiled and said sure. I put it in my pocket and held it almost the entire day. Sign 1. We are exactly where we are supposed to be.

Next, when I entered the meeting room, a member of the Japanese delegation was placing memo pads with *Hello Kitty* on the back table. It was a representation of the kitty that exactly matched the one on the cell phone case my daughter Jacquie had given me for Christmas. I picked up pads for both of us. Sign 2. In a universe that responds to us.

Piotr got back in touch with me. Our plans were set. He would pick me up from the train station in Bratislava at 0930 a few days later. Sign 3. Life after Vienna.

Buoyed by the day's events, I decided to dine

alone in a pub near the hostel, content to sift through my thoughts. I was still unsettled by the fact that I had not felt him thinking of me for the entirety of my time in Vienna. This was very disturbing to me.

Night Twelve

Philippe was running late. His daughter had called, extremely upset in the message she had left him. He had to get home. He raced out of the train station, anxiously jabbing at the phone trying to call her back. He never saw it coming. The truck made the turn on two wheels, hydroplaning in the rain. It hit him head on.

He lay unconscious in the intensive care unit, strung up to monitors and tubes of sustenance, hanging in that place between this plane and the next.

Day Thirteen

It was the last day at the UN. Mike and I were going to La Traviata. Fitting, an opera about love gone wrong, romance denounced for flawed reasons founded in ill-conceived attempts at nobility, the noble denouncer only to die. The *sturm und drang* were not lost on me. I was back in a dark place.

First, Mike and I would go to the top of a local hotel and take in the view. Truly, despite the lowest lows of the two weeks endured there, the experience in Vienna had been a high point for both him and me professionally. We toasted our futures.

And a bit of mine unfolded. I received an email from the Hague Academy. I was accepted into the summer program for Public International Law, a plan first put into motion while my love and I were in close communication back in early December. Well, he might be gone, but it was still a great opportunity. Life would continue.

After a traditional Viennese dinner and a marvelous night at the opera, Mike and I said our farewells. We had been great friends for years; he had done some true combat duty standing by my side during this latest turn of events. I would remember that always.

Night Thirteen

The vision of him unconscious, or worse, dead, was too horrific for me to even close my eyes. I was not willing to risk seeing that again. I called my daughter instead—Jacquie, whose very presence *in utero* was enough to redeem me, so many long years ago when confronted by a more violent abandonment. Jack's suicide.

Our mother/daughter relationship was unusual from conception. I felt the spark of my daughter's life the second she ignited. I dreamed about her in my first trimester. I knew she was female, I knew what she looked like, long before the details surrounding her birth were to play out.

I had always valued the honesty of our communication. There were times when we had blind spots toward each other but when push came to shove, we could talk. Her own motherhood, and the pressures of adulthood, had strewn more gravel into her soul than she had been born with, but her true nature is soft curves, warm and giving. I needed both - her pragmatism and her empathy.

She heard my anguish immediately. "Mom, why aren't you sleeping? What time is it there?" I told her the ongoing story of my nights in Room 7, juxtaposed against the surreal backdrop of days at the UN. I told her about the questions that were driving me round the bend — was any of it real? How had he forsaken me? Why did I care?

She was flabbergasted that I, her stoic mother, the least co-dependent person anyone knew, was still going around and around about this. In her estimation, he had been in one relationship, a pleasant fantasy one, and I had been in quite another, a real one. She was incensed. No one hurt her mother like this.

We talked about my difficulties letting go of Jim, my ex-husband, and the profound differences between that time and this. Then, I hadn't doubted the truth of my perceptions. It was actually my integration of those perceptions which prompted me to divorce Jim. He could never resist an opportunity to seed me with self-doubt. It was his personal mission, breaking me down. Leaving him was my hard-won emancipation. This, on the other hand, was completely different. It had felt so real, I had felt so understood. How could I be so wrong? How could I reconcile then with now?

Jacquie pointed out the many things I was dealing with at this time in my life, my tumor and its concomitant uncertainty, the realities of aging, possible side effects from my medication, the stresses of writing a thesis. She was right. I had to view this in context. It was not happening in a vacuum. More than anything, she said I needed to sleep and get back to running. Writing I had never let go of; my journal was my constant companion in Room 7. When I wasn't struggling with manufactured scenarios, I was chronicling them. But sleep, the lack of sleep — that was as big a factor in my inability to place all of this as the reality of my feelings for the man. She said.

We talked about how wonderful I felt when the connection between him and me was palpable — when the energy between us was something I could sense, not merely something I would think about. She gave me a helpful idea. When I was lying there, unable to sleep, and breathing did not break the mental cycle, she suggested that I send some of that white light to others that were in sore need of it. The fact that I did not know these people shouldn't bother me. I didn't know his mother and I sent her light all the time. Jacquie proceeded to tell me about different people that really needed my help, people who had not spurned me. One in particular touched my heart. She was the very young daughter of the member of a band my daughter and her husband followed. The child had been stricken with a brain tumor and her situation appeared more grim than mine.

And Jacquie told me to give myself credit. I had toughed it out in a rough situation. I had not turned tail and run home. I stayed and I did my work at the UN and no one there knew anything about him, only that someone had done me badly. All assumed that it was someone in Florida. She told me to see myself as the class act I was.

After many hours on the phone, I finally felt like I could handle the rest under my own power. There were only about two hours left before daylight and the time I should get going to catch my train to Bratislava. My daughter had given me gifts to last a lifetime.

I took a last look at my monastic little cell. No frills, so basic, but it had been just what I needed for this difficult period of reckoning, this room where I cried and I sweat and I tossed and turned, while I came to terms with the the reality that he really was out of my life, all the way, at least for the time being.

I was back where I had been before Cape Town. Some of my struggle came from my disappointment that I was so positive and so giving and forgiving and I still did not get my happiness, my fulfillment. I was gaining perspective.

I hailed a cab and set out for Sudbanhof and the train east. I thought about how it was not my will, but that of something/someone greater, with which

I chose to align myself. I must continue to trust that this was all part of the greater good.

No matter what, I was out of Vienna. This hell had a discrete beginning, middle, and end. It was behind me from here.

Bratislava

I started a new volume of my journal - "the rest of my life" — and watched the countryside roll by. The day was grey and bleak but I felt light. I was going somewhere else. After the conversation with Jacquie the night before, I felt like I was ready to put it all behind me. Enough already. What was I hanging on to? Wasn't I cried out by now?

My train got in early and I texted Piotr and took a taxi instead of waiting for him. I got to my hotel and was immediately grateful that I had sprung for the amenities. Yes, enough with the deprivation mentality. The fact that he didn't want me did not mean I had to suffer. I settled into my room, pleased with the marble over-improvement of the bathroom, made all the more so when contrasted against the somewhat mediocre decor of the room. Okay by me. After sharing a shower and bathroom in the hostel for two long weeks, I was ready for some over-the-top.

I had noticed the nearly clear streets on the taxi hop to my hotel. The icy piles on the edges were sufficiently melted that I could easily avoid them. I put on my running gear, hit the gym first for some weights, and then, oh glorious day, I went for my first real run in weeks. I ran and ran, by a cemetery, by a river, who knows where. I had no idea where I was going. I had the foresight to tuck the hotel's business card into my jog bra before I headed out, just in case I got completely turned around. I just kept going. If I couldn't walk for a day or two after this workout, no matter. It was worth the pure exhilaration. And, I knew, there was a better chance I would sleep if I was completely worn out. Somehow, I found my way back to the hotel without incident.

And there, a fantastic breakfast spread awaited

me. Could it get much better than this? Silly pop music from the 80's was piped over the speakers and I couldn't stop smiling. I was beginning to feel like myself again. Piotr and I made a plan via SMS; he would pick me up in an hour. I got myself gussied up.

Piotr is a hunk. We knew each other from our post-grad program. We had always liked each other but never been particularly close. I warned him before coming; I told him that I was heartbroken and gave that as my reason for wanting some me time at the hotel. He was not totally prepared for my condition when he picked me up. This was a bit of a chink in what was the best day I had experienced in a while — I thought I was doing so much better, and, relatively speaking, I was. Still, as he pried and I recounted, the tears began to well.

He listened with the benefit of the male perspective and with far more current serial relationship experience than I had. He thought I should call him, tell him I was coming to Paris next, give him one last chance to make things right. I said that I felt like I could not do this, like he wanted to stay away from me for whatever reason and I wanted to honor that. So, Piotr came up with some other ideas. First, we would tour Bratislava. We would take in the War Memorial, we would go to diiner in the mountains and be serenaded by gypsies. We would go in search of the best *chocolat chaud*. We would end our one day together going to a club with his friends.

And that is what we did. We talked and we laughed and I cried and I ranted. I became thoroughly enamored of the blessing that is good, truly good, thick dark hot chocolate. We ended the night in a club with many bottles of red wine. Piotr asked the dj to play "I Will Survive" and cleared the dance floor. He demanded that I get up and lip synch, claiming it was a necessary part of my therapy. Under duress, kicking and screaming and laughing all the way, I got out on that dance floor and to hell with lip synching. I was belting full out with Gloria Gaynor. It felt so good. By the end of the song I was surrounded by empowered laughing females, shaking it up. I said my good-byes soon after and walked back to my hotel.

And slept. Yes, I slept. I did not sleep long but I

slept hard. I was deep in REM like I had not been in weeks. When my eyes flew open the next day, I felt like it was the first morning in Genesis. I could do anything.

I packed up again, went for run number two and then down to that wonderful breakfast, where I waited for Piotr to come to take me to the train station. I had decided to take the train all the way to Paris. I had time. I would think and read and write. The original plan had been that we would spend a few days in Paris before I headed home. I had already paid for the hotel, close to his apartment. My flight was out of Charles De Gaulle. I gave Piotr my heartfelt thank you and bid him adieu.

I boarded. It was a night train and I slept almost the entire trip. Making up for lost time. By the time I got to Paris, I was convinced that the worst of it was behind me. I did not feel connected to him. I believed he had never loved me, at least not as I had loved him. I was in the City of Lights. I was staying in a nice hotel. I had a facial booked and some pretty cocktail dresses to put on and I was ready to hit the town. Life was better. I felt a bit daunted at the prospect of being in the city where he lived, just a short distance from his home, staying in the hotel where I had thought we would tryst. But I was tough. I could do anything.

Paris

I went for another run, had my facial, and got ready to head out to dinner in Paris, armed with a little black dress, Dolce & Gabbana satin t-straps, and my full-length mink. The girls at the concierge station had befriended me. Despite my bravado, it was clear to anyone with any modicum of depth that I was a woman with a story. They had already gotten from me that I was trying to recover from a heartbreak. I had the entire hotel staff drinking chocolat chaud before the end of my first afternoon there. I enlisted their help in finding a suitable restaurant with live jazz and set out.

I decided to sit at the bar. I could see better and I didn't feel like I was off in Siberia. After fielding the overtures of some truly marginal types, an older, rather rotund man and a very young woman took the stools next to mine. They were father and daughter. Interesting, maybe I could garner some insight. There are clues everywhere.

We had a wonderful time talking. I tried to keep my discussion off of personal matters, but I did allude to the sad fact that I was in Paris because of plans made months before and since broken. Plans that, for whatever stubborn reason, I had decided to leave in place in some ridiculous hope that he would reconsider and get in touch with me after taking time to think about it for the weeks since we had last communicated.

I made loose plans with the girl and her father for the next day; we would rent bikes and tour Paris together. I wanted to visit some markets; they had some places to show me. We exchanged cell phone numbers. I took my leave and caught a cab. When I got to the hotel, I was astonished to discover that the man taken the liberty of following my cab in a separate one. He jumped out, trying to corner me. I brushed past, annoyed and shocked. I got the bell captain to dispense with him. The man proceeded to text me thoroughly inappropriate nonsense, hoping to get together with me. My heart sank. This was what I had to look forward to? My quasi-good spirits deflated and I went to bed.

But, after lying there realizing that he was possibly less than 2 km away from me, if he was not in Bordeaux with his mother, I actually fell asleep for the third night in a row.

Saturday morning heralded my only complete day in Paris. I decided to visit La Defense after a good long run and then I would hit the various markets I wanted to visit. I had a full itinerary. Forget the bike plan. Yuk. I started out, full of energy and ideas. But gradually, as I watched people on the Paris Metro, I began to feel sad. It started to rain. My open air market visits were not sounding like such a fun time anymore. I got off at random stops, just walking around. I had even lost the heart to light candles in churches. At this point, after lighting so many, it felt like overkill.

And then I started seeing images that he had shared with me, places and things he had photographed and sent to me back in better days — musicians in the subway, crazy crowded little side streets, and the fountain, the Niki de Sant Phalle fountain by Centre Pompidou. It was the fountain that did it, that completely unraveled me. All of my bravado was gone by now, all of my brand new certainty that none of it meant anything, that I had dusted myself off and could knee-jerk myself onto new people, places, and things without a backward glance.

When I saw that fountain, I knew that he had loved me. I turned the corner and saw it with his eyes. I took my own picture of it. I was undone. I couldn't see a thing, between my tears and the rain, so I found myself a seat in a cafe and had some tea. This was a completely unexpected turn of events. I could feel him again, with more sensual acuity than I remembered. My skin was prickling. But there it was, there he was. He was in me.

I started to think about my own life. True, I had never had anyone do this to me before, but I had been guilty of similar. I could not deny it. Perhaps this was at the root of my inability to simply drop-kick him to the curb, just write him off as a complete and total jerk.

Yes, I had done this, this stonewalling, this silence, this falling off the grid completely – twice before in my life. Maybe this was my karma. Maybe understanding who I was, and the complicated cir-cumstances of my life at those times, could help me understand what he might be going through. There is only one of us here. We are all of us connected by biology and drive and need and want and striving to be, to find, better.

I did not know what had happened. Perhaps I would never know. But by now I knew it could have been what he said – that his life got complicated and then maybe he didn't want to encourage me. It could have been any of those all too plausible scenarios that had thrashed around my psyche. While I wished that he had just talked honestly to me, as a person, he had chosen not to. It would have made it so much easier for me to just put it all to rest. There was nothing he could have told me that I could not have handled. But, since he hadn't, there must be a lesson here. These were the cards I had been dealt.

I was 26 years old the first time I had done this. When I met my daughter's father, Jack, I was married to someone else. I got married when I was in boot camp, to a guy who was getting shipped out to the Philippines. It was a win:win. He was trying to avoid a woman and I was trying to put layers between myself, and a very bad ex-boyfriend who had a lot of money and power and a penchant for hitting me. I thought getting married would protect me. Darryl and I never lived together; we had a wild weekend and went off and got married and he shipped out. I went to NAS Meridian in MS and met Jack and fell in love.

I drove across the country to California when Darryl's ship finally came in, nearly a year later. I went to tell him about Jack and my pregnancy. When I got there, his family was so nice to me and he was all pumped up with hopeful plans for his future with this cute girl he had married (me). I didn't know how to bring up the subject. I went through two days of pure hell.

Finally, the second night, while he was sleeping, I just got up and left in the middle of the night. Yes, I slunk out like a wet cat. No note. No explanation. I just left and went back to Jack in Meridian. Darryl looked all over for me, called my father's house, couldn't locate me, got drunk and went riding on his motorcycle. He wrecked it and he messed up his very handsome face. Jack ended his life, for other reasons. I felt horrible about both and still did. I remembered all too well how awful it was to not know what to say.

The second time I did this was near the end of my marriage to Jim, right before he moved out. Jim was unfaithful to me. I lived with it. I looked the other way. I traveled a lot and for a while it didn't affect me terribly. Eventually, he started being disrespectful and doing it under my nose and it hurt and it pissed me off. Big time. I decided to teach him a lesson. I told him I was going to but he didn't believe me. So,

I had an affair. Yes, I would go have a liaison with my paramour and then go home and crawl into bed with my husband. Not nice at all. I carried on like this for a short time (about a month and a half), completely shocked at the ease with which I could lie and cover my tracks.

Steve, the other guy, was busy making big plans for us. He saw a nice house and a girl with good income-earning potential and maybe he cared, maybe he didn't, but he was moving way too fast for me. My daughter, then 15, was in complete shock about her parents' breakup. She knew about Steve. She also knew her Dad was no angel but I was her rock and she was shaken and very unhappy.

I was close to getting Jim to move out of the house and Steve was working hard to move in and I did not want the reasons for the end of my marriage to Jim to get lost in this new thing with this new guy who, for all his enthusiasm, I was not too sure about. The more Steve pushed, the further away I wanted to go. It was very important to me that Jim understand that our marriage was not ending because of a relationship with this other guy. Our problems had nothing to do with anyone but us. And, I knew that I needed to just let the dust settle, Jacquie and I were in shell shock. I felt completely awful about cheating on Jim.

By this time I knew that I didn't feel anything for Steve beyond flattery for his attention and I knew that I really loved my husband even though he had pierced my heart with knives. I realized our marriage was over. Still, I wasn't going to throw Jim out quickly or coldly and I knew that I was going to take my own god damn sweet time on everything. But I didn't know how to tell Steve that. So I just did nothing. I stopped taking his calls, I stopped answering his emails. I went silent. I simply didn't know what to say to him. Ultimately, he married a friend of mine and I made amends to him and we made our peace. Certainly a better ending than the other story.

I was beginning to remember how truly complicated life could be. I already knew that good people could be capable of less than stellar behavior.

Tears were streaming down my face. I felt complete forgiveness for him. He was just a person, doing his best. That was all. I forgave myself.

I thought about the two sides to the rabbit hole of my thoughts: the up side where I had deluded myself into false hope, naively thinking that he would just show up in Vienna and we would fall into each others arms. And the down side, where I tortured myself with all those unverifiable variations of events. Each was a form of delusion. Neither had much to do with observable fact. I thought about the night I had come to appreciate the empirical data contained in my perceptions. I had to trust myself. I had to control my thoughts. They were as fickle as feelings. Truly, my best compass would be my perceptions.

The rain had stopped. I took the Metro back to the hotel. The girls at the concierge desk were worried about me. It was clear that I had been crying, hard. We had more *chocolat chaud* and worked on my dinner plans. I decided that I wanted to be treated like a queen, the Queen of Everything, catered to. Michelin-rated or bust. They set to task, looking for a suitable venue which is daunting on a Saturday night in Paris. All the good places are closed. But, they found me one and made me a reservation. I had a few hours to patch up my face.

I managed to pull myself together and I looked reasonably good, all things considered. I don't know what the concierge told the restaurant staff, but I have never been treated better. The food was like artwork, the wines were subtle and delicate and complex. I was marginally snockered by the time I got back to the hotel. I hung out in the bar with the gay bartender who was nursing his own broken heart, playing him songs from that fateful Christmas compilation which was stored on my iPhone. I concocted a plan. I was leaving the next morning. I knew where he lived. His address was easily accessible in the French White Pages on the Internet. I mapped it on my iPhone. It was ridiculously close. I would run there in the morning.

After a few hours of sleep, I took off in the 0500 dark, my favorite time to run. The air was crisp, the sky was clear, there were few people out. The streets were dirty, but it was French dirt. It looked artistic.

I ran by the Arc. My heart was pounding.

I slowed to a walk. I wanted to absorb as much as I could, the sights, the sounds, during my favorite pre-dawn morning light, getting a sense of his neighborhood, the place he called home, the streets he ran, the places he walked his dog.

I found his address. I stood in front of his building and I had the most profound sense of peace wash over me. I sensed the reality of all he shared and all he left unsaid, the gravitas of his obligations and I just sent him my love, my energy, but from right outside his window, not half a world away.

That I didn't make contact in the material world did not matter to me at all. Somehow, I understood what a gift I gave him by not pushing the issue, by not forcing a confrontation, by not contacting him and making him feel worse than he already did. I did something purely unselfish, because his peace meant more to me than my suffering.

I realized that I had finally grown up where love is concerned. It wasn't all about me. I thought about my youngest brother's favorite definition of love, extending yourself for the benefit of another with no thought of benefit for yourself. I was there.

I thought about all of those horrible scenarios and whether I would ever know what happened. I realized that I did know this much. I was going home. I had more certainty in that, much more, than I had had in a long time. I knew what to expect of my life and that was that it was a safe harbor. I knew that I would nurse myself back to health and I would create and I would do the scut work of my thesis in order to lay the foundation for its message. I knew that I would take care of my dogs.

I knew that I would love my morning runs and my evening fires. I would help my daughter and my brothers and my friends. Maybe I would write to him someday, I did not yet know. But whatever had happened, it had not occurred because of us. There had never been anything ugly between us, only profound connection, intense desire, idealistic dreams. Never, an unkind word.

I knew that I believed in the magic of what we shared. I did not know what tomorrow might bring where he was concerned but I did know that I had done nothing to hurt its chances. I knew that I wanted only peace and happiness and health and blessings for him.

I thought about all the things that I had endured in Vienna and what I had learned as a result. I had learned that sometimes positive mental attitude and sweetness and decency were not enough to ensure that I would get what I wanted, that it was hard to concentrate when my heart was breaking, and that I could be discreet anyway. I learned that for all that this was hurting I was still glad to have met him. I had no regrets. I had learned that breathing was my anchor. I had learned to control my thoughts.

I had discovered that sharing my innermost self felt wonderful, even at this price. That love does, indeed, make the world go round. I learned that I wanted more than what I had ever had with anyone before. I wanted to share my soul. I was no longer willing to isolate myself like I had been for years. I wanted that spark, that immediate sense of knowing that something is important.

I looked at his building. I was crying. It was still dark. I wondered if he could feel me outside, if his senses were as attuned to mine as mine were to his. I thought about how I had come so far, was so close, and yet I had no desire to try to make contact. This was enough.

Sometimes the pain of love is necessary to shape the joy of love, it gives it dimension. My feelings for him had so much more texture for going through all of this, for suffering without him, but finally coming to this place, where I bore him only kind and patient understanding.

We were exactly where we were supposed to be right now and that was not together. I could not do anything about that, but I realized I also could not do anything about the fact that I still loved him like I breathed. It would not go away simply because we did not speak or because we did not see each other. When I met him I had woken up. That did not evaporate because I didn't get what I wanted. But, more important, I had shown up, all the way. I loved who I had been, how I had been during the entire interaction. The whys and wherefores of his behavior had no real impact upon the truth and purity of my emotion and my actions. I would take that with me wherever I went from that place forward.

I knew that I would always love that part of him with which I had connected, no matter what, no matter where we ended up or who we ended up with. What it came down to was faith, that what is real is, ultimately, always real.

I also realized that I owed it to myself to live a happy life, with or without him. That didn't detract from the connection, which while gone in Vienna was now back in full force. But I could not wait to get home, to my beautiful, full, productive, purposeful life.

The Paris light was changing with the dawn. I knew that I was in no way diminished by this experience. My life was forever changed. The encounter had brought out the best parts of my self. I was deeper, truer, realer, better. What a gift. He had not broken my heart. He had broken it open.

I squared my shoulders as I squared the corner,

turning on my heel to head back to my hotel, the
airport, the States, ready for the next installment of
my grand adventure.

Sound off, 1, 2
Sound off, 3, 4
Sound off, 1,2, 3, 4
1, 2, 3, 4

left, your left. left, right, right on left.

Mama, mama can't you see?
Mama, mama can't you see?
what true love has done to me?
what true love has done to me?
Mama, mama can't you see?
Mama, mama can't you see?
tore me loose and set me free,
tore me loose and set me free.

20 June 2012
Eva Bianca
Evora, Portugal

ABOUT THE AUTHOR

Eva Bianca is a legal academic who specializes in the law of commercial activities in outer space. She writes under a pen name to protect the privacy of the people whose stories she shares in these pages. She divides her time between Europe and the United States.